The Great Chapatti Chase

Written by Penny Dolan

Illustrated by Laura Sua

Collins

Long ago and faraway, in a village in India,
a woman walked wearily home from the well.
"And now it's time to make my bread," she said
with a sigh, going into her small kitchen. She threw
some handfuls of flour into a tin bowl, poured in
a trickle of cool water and kneaded it all together
to make some dough.

Pop! She placed a small piece between the palms of her hands. Round and round she rolled that dough, making a small round ball.

Then she placed the ball on a square wooden board, took her little rolling pin and set to work.

The woman rolled the dough flat and turned it, again and again, until she had made a perfectly round chapatti.

The woman smiled. "My, what a handsome little chapatti," she said. "You'll be delicious to eat!" And – flip, flap! – she flung that chapatti on to the hot iron stove.

However – believe it or not! – as soon as this little chapatti felt the fire, he puffed out his fat round cheeks and grinned.

"Delicious to eat?" he replied, laughing. "No, no, you silly woman! I'm not staying to be eaten!"

With that, he jumped off the stove and rolled right out of the door, singing for all to hear:
"*Run, run as fast as you can! You can't catch me, I'm Chapatti Man!*"

"Come back!" the woman cried. She chased after him, with all her bangles jangling. "Come back!" called her children, running as fast as they could, but not one was swift enough to catch up with that cheeky little chapatti.

After a while, the chapatti came to a weaver's hut.
A watchful cat crouched on a tall stack of carpets.
As the little chapatti rolled by, she jumped down.

"Stop, stop! You look good to eat!" she mewed.

"Eat me, you fluffy fleabag? No, no!" the little chapatti answered. He rolled right out of the yard, singing: *"Run, run as fast as you can. You can't catch me, I'm Chapatti Man!"*

The cat raced after him, her fur all in a frizz, but she was just not fast enough.

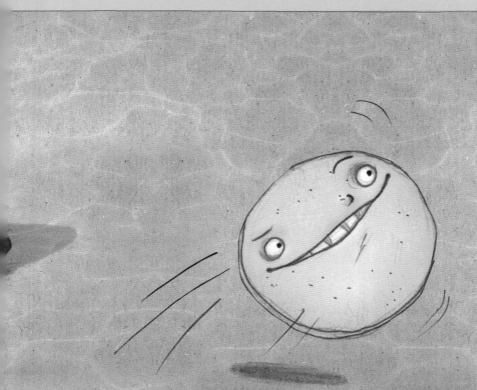

Before long, the chapatti came to a busy market.
A dog lay dozing under a stall. As the little chapatti
rolled by, he lept up, tail wagging with excitement.

"Stop, stop! You look good to eat!" he yelped.

"Huh! Do you think I'd let myself be eaten by a silly dog like you?" the little chapatti answered, rolling right past, and singing: *"Run, run as fast as you can. You can't catch me, I'm Chapatti Man!"*

The dog ran, barking, after the runaway, but soon he gave up too.

On down the road rolled that little chapatti.

After a while, he came across an elderly goat, nibbling the grass by the roadside. She stopped chewing when she saw the little chapatti rolling by.

"Stop, stop! You look good to eat!" she bleated. "Come here!"

"No way! You're not nibbling me, you giddy goat!"
laughed the little chapatti. He rolled right past her,
singing: *"Run, run as fast as you can! You can't catch
me, I'm Chapatti Man!"*

The goat tried trotting after him, but the long
halter round her neck held her back.

On rolled the little chapatti man, chuckling
to himself.

A brown cow came wandering along the road.
She stared as the little chapatti came rolling
towards her.

"Stop, stop, you look good to eat!" she mooed.

"No, no! Why should I be munched up by you, you lazy lump?" the little chapatti answered and away he rolled, singing: *"Run, run as fast as you can. You can't catch me, I'm Chapatti Man!"*

The cow charged after him, with the bell on her collar clanging loudly. Quite soon, she grew weary, and sat herself down by the road to rest.

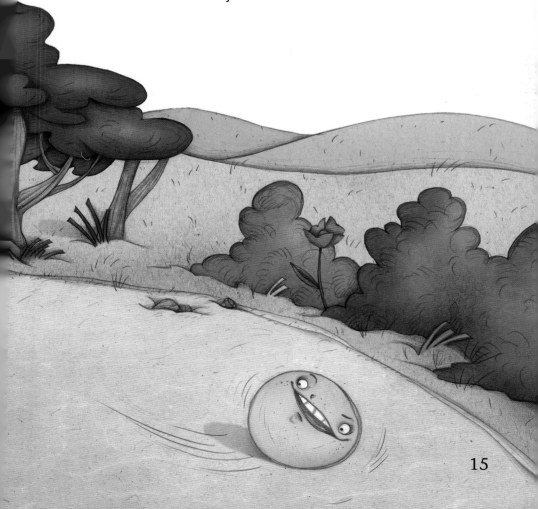

Eventually, the little chapatti rolled towards a fine country house. A magnificent elephant was waiting outside, ready for a procession.

"Stop, stop, you look good to eat!" the elephant trumpeted, raising her trunk and flapping her big ears.

"I'm not stopping for you, big fancy face!" called the little chapatti, chuckling.

He rolled right on, singing: *"Run, run as fast as you can. You can't catch me, I'm Chapatti Man!"*

The elephant ran after him, with all her ornaments swaying, and all the people shouting, but soon even she came to a halt.

The little chapatti rolled on and on into a forest.
After a while, the path led him down to the banks
of a wide river.

"Bother, bother! How can I get across?" he cried.
"I don't want to end up soggy and wet."

"You poor thing!" purred a soft voice.
"Maybe I can help you?"

The little chapatti looked up and saw a handsome
tiger stretched out along the branch of a tree.
The tiger yawned, clambered lazily down, and gave
an enormous smile.

"Little Chapatti Man, I can't bear to see you in trouble. If you sat on my tail, I could carry you across the water," he said. "Tigers are very good at swimming."

"Thank you, dear, kind Tiger!" cried the little chapatti. Without a thought, he jumped – flip flap! – on to the tiger's tail.

Tiger swam seven strokes, but gradually his striped tail began to droop.

"Help! The water is closer," squeaked the little chapatti.

"Sorry, little Chapatti Man. My tail feels rather tired today. Why don't you roll up on to my back?"

So the chapatti did just that.

When Tiger reached the middle of the river, he swam so very slowly that the water lapped against his furry sides.

"Take care, Tiger! The water is even closer," squealed the little chapatti.

"Dear Chapatti Man, my paws are not as strong at swimming as I thought. Why don't you hop up between my ears?"

So that is just what the little chapatti did.

This time, the tiger swam so slow and low that
the river splish-splashed around his neck and head.

"Friend Tiger, may I climb on to your nose?"
squeaked the little chapatti. "The water is very
near indeed."

"Do, my dear friend, do," said the tiger.
"Roll up there right away. I hope my whiskers
don't tickle you."

So that's just what the little chapatti did.
He rolled right up on to the tiger's nose.

The little chapatti stood proudly, watching
the river bank get closer.

"We're nearly there!" he cried.

Then, suddenly he noticed that the tiger's smile
was much wider than before.